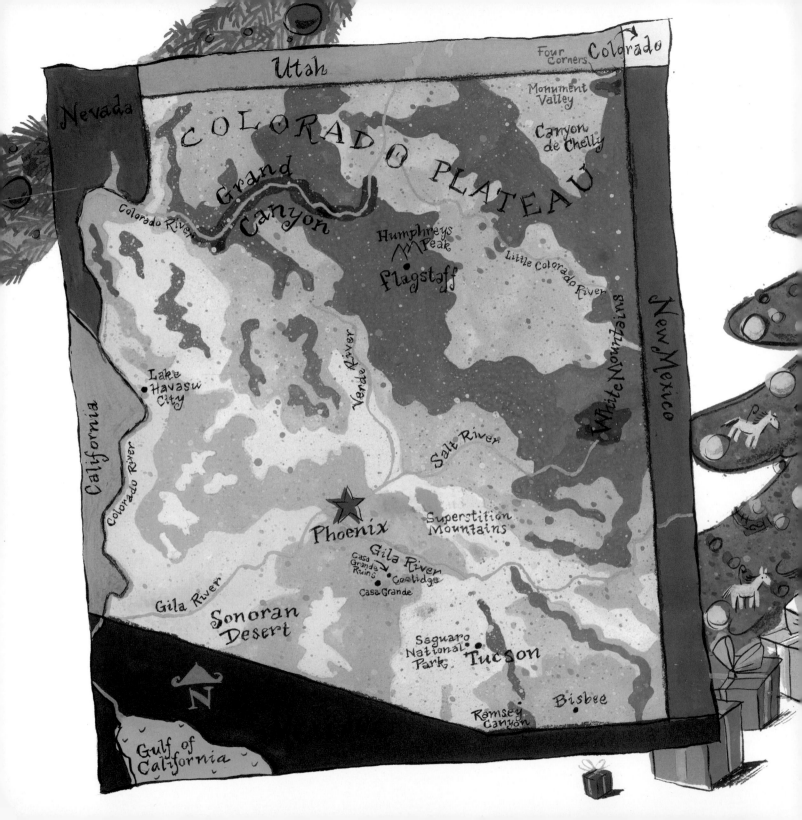

The Twelve Days of Christmas in Arizona

written by
Jennifer J. Stewart

illustrated by
Lynne Avril

STERLING CHILDREN'S BOOKS
New York

Dear Isabella,

¡Feliz Navidad! Do you like surprises? I sure hope so, because I've got a big one planned: You're coming to spend your Christmas vacation in Arizona!

I know, I know, you're used to having a white Christmas. But even if there's no snow where I live, there are still plenty of ways to celebrate the season, Arizona style. You'll see what I mean when you get here. Grandpa and I have mapped out a road trip, with plenty of cool things to see and do, and some more surprises—including one I hope you'll think is REALLY grand. We're going to have lots of fun! Here's your plane ticket, so you can start packing.

¡Hasta la vista! Until I see you, which will be soon!

Your favorite cousin,
Carlos

P.S. Don't forget your sunglasses!

Dear Mom and Papá,

Hola from Arizona!! Carlos and Grandpa met me at the Tucson airport. Grandpa grabbed my suitcase from the luggage carousel, and off we went. At Carlos's house, lots of relatives were waiting to welcome me with a <u>fiesta</u>!

On the patio, I noticed a strange tree with pale green bark. Carlos told me it was a <u>palo verde</u>. That means "green stick," and it's the state tree. If it doesn't rain for a long time, the <u>palo verde</u> can lose all its tiny leaves and still do its photosynthesis thing. How cool is that?! Wait until I tell my science teacher!

As we were hanging the <u>piñata</u>, a funny, speckled bird scolded us, sounding like Grandpa's truck when it doesn't want to start. Turns out she's a cactus wren, the state bird! Carlos showed me her nests. That's right, she doesn't have just one. She builds a bunch of fake nests to protect her babies. That's one smart bird!

After I was blindfolded, I swung at the <u>piñata</u> with a stick. I missed twice, but on the third swing I gave it a good whack, and then it was raining candy!

We'll set out on our road trip tomorrow. I can hardly wait!

Love,
Isabella

On the first day of Christmas,
my cousin gave to me . . .

a cactus wren
in a palo verde.

Dear Mom and Papá,

Our first stop was Saguaro National Park. The saguaro is the biggest cactus in the world. I'm talking GIGANTIC! It grows sloooowly from a tiny seed. Grandpa says saguaros don't grow any arms until they're as old as he is, which is 70. Even then they're not done growing. Some live over 200 years.

Gila woodpeckers will drill holes in saguaros to make nests. Then, when they move out, other birds move in, like a sleepy elf owl Carlos found. Carlos is good at finding things.

The ranger showed us how she tracks wildlife with radio transmitters. Carlos and I followed the signal to two desert tortoises that came out of hibernation just to meet me! We stayed quiet—we didn't want to scare them. It is a really special thing to see them in the wild.

The ranger said if you build a burrow, you can get certified to adopt a desert tortoise. I wish I could, but the Sonoran Desert is the tortoises' home—they wouldn't be happy anywhere else.

The two tortoises went back to their burrows for a long nap. Grandpa said it should be called the "Snorin' Desert."

Love,
Isabella

On the second day of Christmas,
my cousin gave to me . . .

2 tortoises

and a cactus wren in a palo verde.

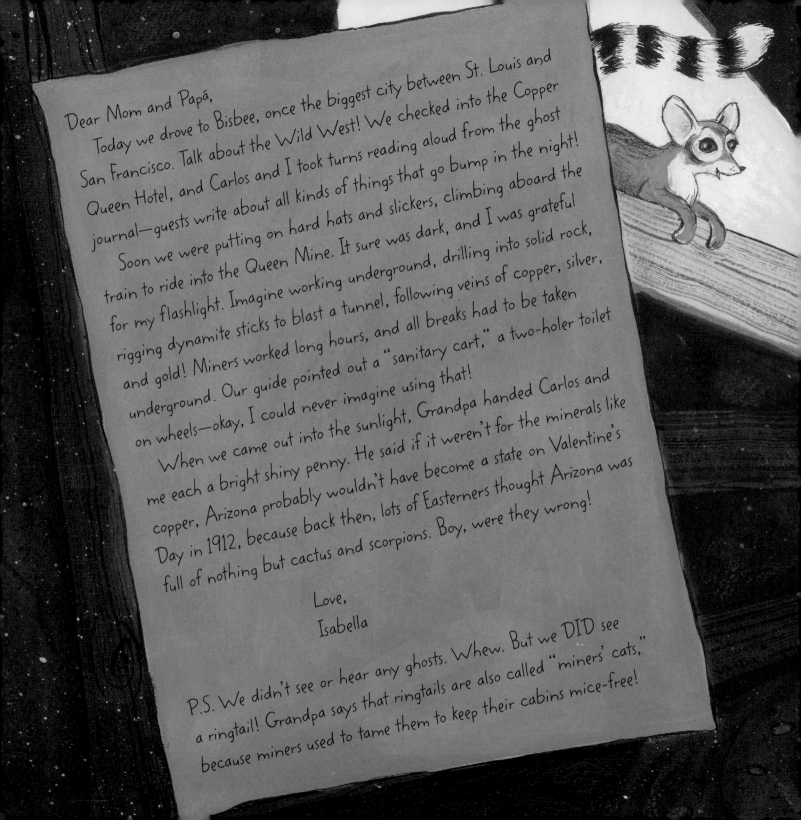

Dear Mom and Papá,

Today we drove to Bisbee, once the biggest city between St. Louis and San Francisco. Talk about the Wild West! We checked into the Copper Queen Hotel, and Carlos and I took turns reading aloud from the ghost journal—guests write about all kinds of things that go bump in the night!

Soon we were putting on hard hats and slickers, climbing aboard the train to ride into the Queen Mine. It sure was dark, and I was grateful for my flashlight. Imagine working underground, drilling into solid rock, rigging dynamite sticks to blast a tunnel, following veins of copper, silver, and gold! Miners worked long hours, and all breaks had to be taken underground. Our guide pointed out a "sanitary cart," a two-holer toilet on wheels—okay, I could never imagine using that!

When we came out into the sunlight, Grandpa handed Carlos and me each a bright shiny penny. He said if it weren't for the minerals like copper, Arizona probably wouldn't have become a state on Valentine's Day in 1912, because back then, lots of Easterners thought Arizona was full of nothing but cactus and scorpions. Boy, were they wrong!

Love,
Isabella

P.S. We didn't see or hear any ghosts. Whew. But we DID see a ringtail! Grandpa says that ringtails are also called "miners' cats," because miners used to tame them to keep their cabins mice-free!

On the third day of Christmas,
my cousin gave to me . . .

3 hard hats

2 tortoises,
and a cactus wren in a palo verde.

Dear Mom and Papá,

Grandpa said he had a humdinger of an idea, so this morning we zipped on over to the Ramsey Canyon Preserve, noted for its wildlife. We hiked the Hamburg Trail along the creek, and I spied a troop of coatis—so cute with their long noses and even longer, faintly striped tails. At the overlook, four hummingbirds buzzed around me, their wings a blur. They must have thought I was a flower.

Did you know hummingbirds can fly forward, backward, and straight up and down? They can even perform somersaults in the air!

Those acrobatics mean hummingbirds have to eat all day long. They sip nectar from flowers and eat bugs for protein. If you fill a feeder, you can watch them sip. The nectar recipe is easy: stir one part sugar with four parts water until the sugar dissolves, and fill the feeder. Do you think we can get hummers to come visit our house?

At night, when hummingbirds sleep, their heart rate slows way down, like they're hibernating. Isn't that cool? And get this: They can even <u>sleep</u> upside down.

Come spring, when the mama hummingbird builds her nest, she adds spiderweb silk for strength so that the nest will stretch as her babies grow. She usually lays two eggs the size of beans. When those babies are born, they look like raisins, but by the time they are three weeks old, they're ready to fly off on their own.

Love,
Isabella

On the fourth day of Christmas,
my cousin gave to me . . .

4 hummingbirds

3 hard hats, 2 tortoises,
and a cactus wren in a palo verde.

Dear Mom and Papá,

On the way north to explore the Casa Grande Ruins National Monument, Grandpa asked if anyone was hungry. Carlos always is, and I was, too, so we stopped at a Mexican restaurant in Coolidge. I just about dove into the chips and salsa the waitress brought us. I tried a <u>chimichanga</u>, because Grandpa said they were invented right here in Arizona. My <u>chimi</u> had spicy beef all wrapped up in a tortilla, then deep fried so that the tortilla gets all flaky. There was sour cream and guacamole on top. Then for dessert, we shared <u>sopapillas</u>! They're like pillows of fried dough, and you fill up the hollow part with honey. I had to stop after two, because by then <u>I</u> was all filled up!

While we were eating, a mariachi band began playing for us. When the trumpets—<u>trompetas</u>—started playing the melody, I felt like getting up and dancing! Grandpa explained that mariachi music originally came from Mexico. Part of Arizona used to belong to Mexico before the United States bought it. Carlos joked that we'd all be speaking Spanish if it were still that way— of course, he speaks Spanish <u>and</u> English. LOTS of people in Arizona are bilingual.

Can I be a singer in a mariachi band when I grow up?

<u>Con amor,</u>
Isabella

On the fifth day of Christmas,
my cousin gave to me . . .

5 golden horns

4 hummingbirds, 3 hard hats, 2 tortoises,
and a cactus wren in a palo verde.

Dear Mom and Papá,

In Phoenix (which is the state capital), the Heard Museum was hosting their annual "Holidays at the Heard" event, with music and dance performances, artist demonstrations, and fry bread!

Did you know there are over 20 American Indian communities in Arizona? Many have a long tradition of making beautiful handmade items. We talked to some of the artists about how they make their crafts.

I'm so glad I left extra room in my suitcase! First, Grandpa bought me a Hopi katsina doll. These dolls are carved from cottonwood root and are given to young girls as gifts. I also picked out a Pascua Yaqui Pascola mask. It is the face of a goat, painted and decorated with horsehair eyebrows and a beard! Then I chose a Zuni animal fetish carved from stone—it took me a long time to decide which animal I wanted. My fourth keepsake is a small Maricopa pottery bowl. I also got a Navajo turquoise and silver bracelet and a Tohono O'odham basket woven from beargrass and yucca.

I can't wait to tell you the stories and meanings behind each one of my treasures!

Love,
Isabella

On the sixth day of Christmas,
my cousin gave to me . . .

6 handmade treasures

5 golden horns,
4 hummingbirds, 3 hard hats, 2 tortoises,
and a cactus wren in a palo verde.

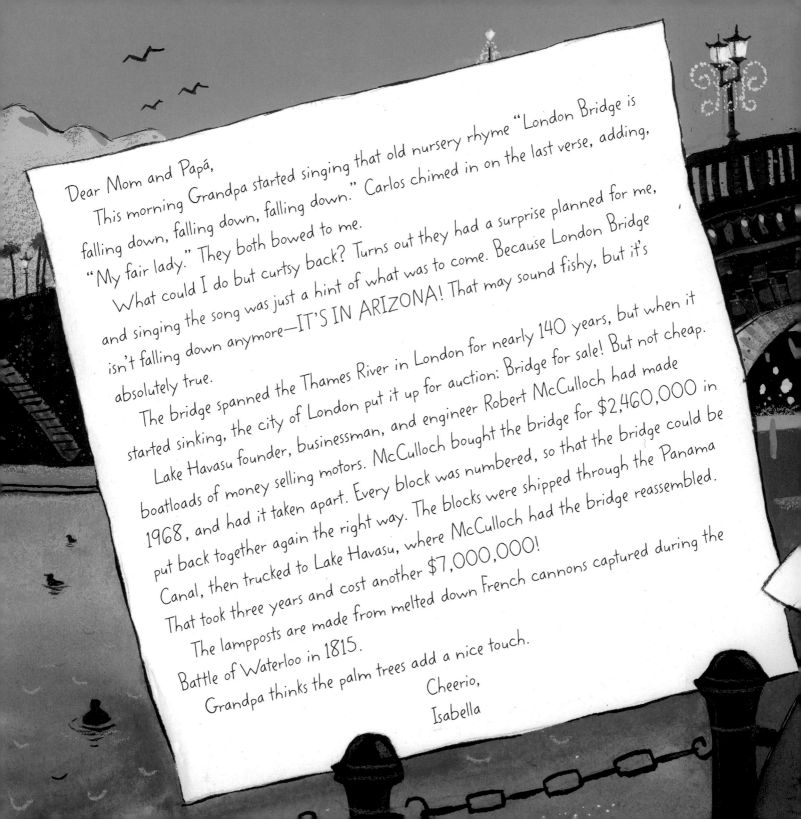

Dear Mom and Papá,

This morning Grandpa started singing that old nursery rhyme "London Bridge is falling down, falling down, falling down." Carlos chimed in on the last verse, adding, "My fair lady." They both bowed to me.

What could I do but curtsy back? Turns out they had a surprise planned for me, and singing the song was just a hint of what was to come. Because London Bridge isn't falling down anymore—IT'S IN ARIZONA! That may sound fishy, but it's absolutely true.

The bridge spanned the Thames River in London for nearly 140 years, but when it started sinking, the city of London put it up for auction: Bridge for sale! But not cheap. Lake Havasu founder, businessman, and engineer Robert McCulloch had made boatloads of money selling motors. McCulloch bought the bridge for $2,460,000 in 1968, and had it taken apart. Every block was numbered, so that the bridge could be put back together again the right way. The blocks were shipped through the Panama Canal, then trucked to Lake Havasu, where McCulloch had the bridge reassembled. That took three years and cost another $7,000,000!

The lampposts are made from melted down French cannons captured during the Battle of Waterloo in 1815.

Grandpa thinks the palm trees add a nice touch.

Cheerio,
Isabella

On the seventh day of Christmas, my cousin gave to me . . .

7 fish a-jumping

6 handmade treasures, 5 golden horns,
4 hummingbirds, 3 hard hats, 2 tortoises,
and a cactus wren in a palo verde.

Dear Mom and Papá,

Scope this out! Today we toured Lowell Observatory in Flagstaff. It's named for Percival Lowell, who set up his telescope here in 1894 to get away from city lights. You can still see a frying pan used as a cap to keep dust off the lens. I bet the cook got mad when someone took the skillet from the kitchen without asking!

Lowell is famous for believing that Mars held intelligent life, but he also predicted the existence of a ninth planet. Of course, no one's ever found any little green men, but in 1930, when young astronomical researcher Clyde Tombaugh was comparing images he'd taken at the observatory, he noticed that one object had moved—that object turned out to be Pluto!

For many years, Pluto was considered to be the ninth planet. But it was much further out than the other eight planets, and its orbit was off-kilter, too. Now most scientists think Pluto isn't really a planet. Instead, it's part of the faraway Kuiper Belt. Today, Lowell astronomers are still making discoveries, trying to figure out how our solar system formed.

Too bad for poor Pluto! Still, it was fun to learn how astronomical discoveries happen. Arizona's clear skies make for some out-of-this-world stargazing.

Love,
Isabella

On the eighth day of Christmas, my cousin gave to me . . .

8 planets whirling

7 fish a-jumping, 6 handmade treasures,
5 golden horns, 4 hummingbirds,
3 hard hats, 2 tortoises,
and a cactus wren in a palo verde.

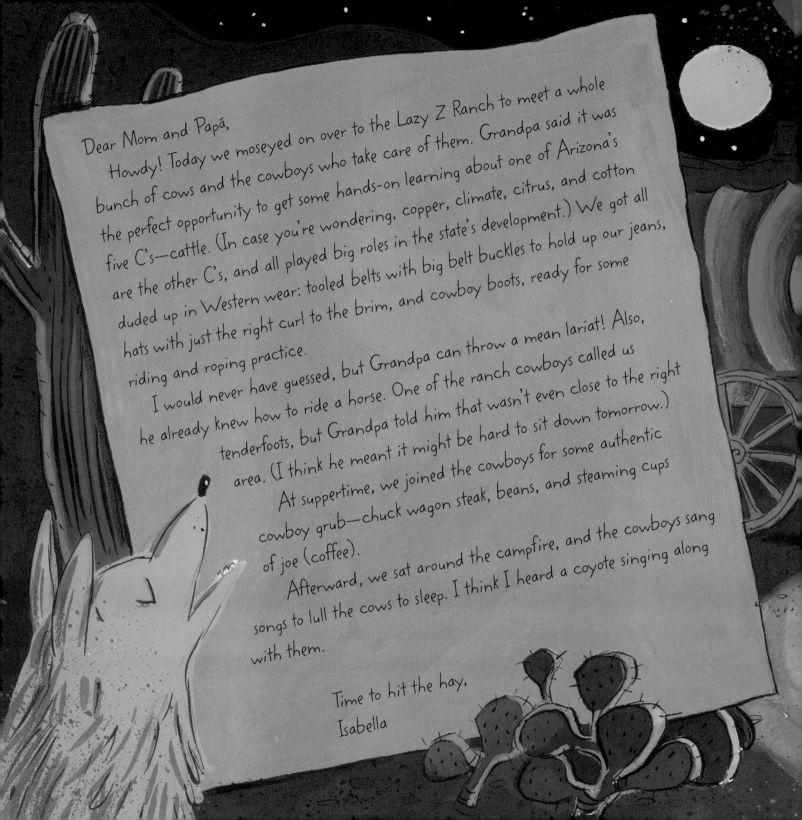

Dear Mom and Papá,

Howdy! Today we moseyed on over to the Lazy Z Ranch to meet a whole bunch of cows and the cowboys who take care of them. Grandpa said it was the perfect opportunity to get some hands-on learning about one of Arizona's five C's—cattle. (In case you're wondering, copper, climate, citrus, and cotton are the other C's, and all played big roles in the state's development.) We got all duded up in Western wear: tooled belts with big belt buckles to hold up our jeans, hats with just the right curl to the brim, and cowboy boots, ready for some riding and roping practice.

I would never have guessed, but Grandpa can throw a mean lariat! Also, he already knew how to ride a horse. One of the ranch cowboys called us tenderfoots, but Grandpa told him that wasn't even close to the right area. (I think he meant it might be hard to sit down tomorrow.)

At suppertime, we joined the cowboys for some authentic cowboy grub—chuck wagon steak, beans, and steaming cups of joe (coffee).

Afterward, we sat around the campfire, and the cowboys sang songs to lull the cows to sleep. I think I heard a coyote singing along with them.

Time to hit the hay,
Isabella

On the ninth day of Christmas, my cousin gave to me . . .

9 cowboys singing

8 planets whirling, 7 fish a-jumping, 6 handmade treasures,
5 golden horns, 4 hummingbirds, 3 hard hats, 2 tortoises,
and a cactus wren in a palo verde.

Dear Mom and Papá,

Today we visited Canyon de Chelly, in the heart of the Navajo Nation, whose members call themselves the Diné. We drove to the overlook to see Spider Rock, a stone spire over 800 feet high.

"Who do you think lives up there?" Grandpa asked.

"Spider-Man," Carlos said. "You'd have to be Spider-Man to live there."

Grandpa laughed. "Close! It's actually Spider Woman who lives at the top of Spider Rock. And she has nada to do with your comic books." He explained that long ago, Spider Woman, a person sacred to the Diné, taught them the art of weaving on a loom. More than yarn is woven into their beautiful rugs—also memories and history, even prayers and pictures.

"So every rug is a gift?" I finally asked.

"Everything they make," Grandpa agreed.

After our hike to the White House Ruins, we headed for Thunderbird Lodge. When Grandpa stopped to look at his map, a bunch of sheep ran by. They were special sheep whose wool will be spun into yarn for Navajo rugs!

At the lodge, we finally got to see the world famous rugs up close—so dazzling you would never ever think of walking on them! People who buy them hang them on their walls just like a painting.

Love,
Isabella

On the tenth day of Christmas,
my cousin gave to me . . .

10 sheep a-leaping

9 cowboys singing, 8 planets whirling,
7 fish a-jumping, 6 handmade treasures, 5 golden horns,
4 hummingbirds, 3 hard hats, 2 tortoises,
and a cactus wren in a palo verde.

Dear Mom and Papá,

Today it was my turn to surprise Carlos. I knew that Carlos had never played in deep snow because it hardly ever snows in Tucson, and when it does, it melts fast. So Grandpa and I cooked up a plan to fix that—we took Carlos sledding! The Wing Mountain Snow Play Area had fresh powder, and some of our new friends showed up, too! The cowboys had more trouble steering their sleds than their horses! Luckily they managed to avoid hitting any trees.

Carlos and I had a snowball fight, too. Playing softball definitely helps my aim!

Grandpa pointed out Humphreys Peak, off in the distance. It's the tallest mountain in Arizona: 12,633 feet tall. Grandpa says if I come back in the summer, maybe we can hike it, all the way to the top.

After we were done, we unfroze our insides with hot chocolate. Mmmm . . . I just love those mini marshmallows. Carlos and I both think they look just like little snowballs.

Love,
Isabella

On the eleventh day of Christmas,
my cousin gave to me . . .

11 sleds a-sliding

10 sheep a-leaping, 9 cowboys singing, 8 planets whirling,
7 fish a-jumping, 6 handmade treasures, 5 golden horns,
4 hummingbirds, 3 hard hats, 2 tortoises,
and a cactus wren in a palo verde.

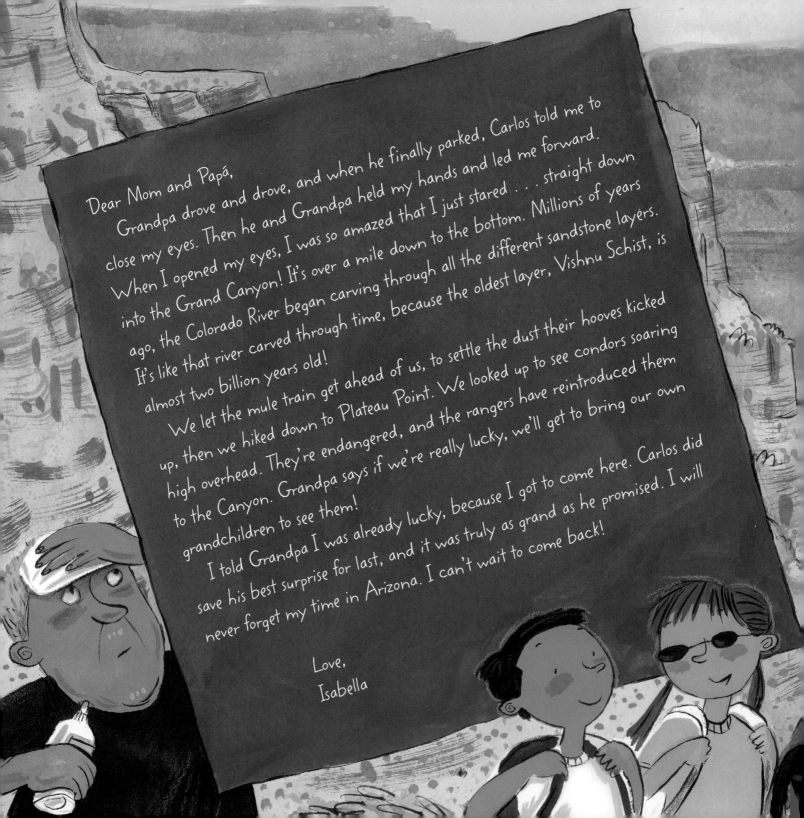

Dear Mom and Papá,

Grandpa drove and drove, and when he finally parked, Carlos told me to close my eyes. Then he and Grandpa held my hands and led me forward. When I opened my eyes, I was so amazed that I just stared . . . straight down into the Grand Canyon! It's over a mile down to the bottom. Millions of years ago, the Colorado River began carving through all the different sandstone layers. It's like that river carved through time, because the oldest layer, Vishnu Schist, is almost two billion years old!

We let the mule train get ahead of us, to settle the dust their hooves kicked up, then we hiked down to Plateau Point. We looked up to see condors soaring high overhead. They're endangered, and the rangers have reintroduced them to the Canyon. Grandpa says if we're really lucky, we'll get to bring our own grandchildren to see them!

I told Grandpa I was already lucky, because I got to come here. Carlos did save his best surprise for last, and it was truly as grand as he promised. I will never forget my time in Arizona. I can't wait to come back!

Love,
Isabella

On the twelfth day of Christmas,
my cousin gave to me . . .

12 mules a-hauling

11 sleds a-sliding, 10 sheep a-leaping,
9 cowboys singing, 8 planets whirling,
7 fish a-jumping, 6 handmade treasures,
5 golden horns, 4 hummingbirds,
3 hard hats, 2 tortoises,
and a cactus wren in a palo verde.

Arizona: The Grand Canyon State

Capital: Phoenix • **State abbreviation:** AZ • **Largest city:** Phoenix • **State bird:** the cactus wren • **State flower:** the saguaro blossom • **State tree:** the palo verde • **State fossil:** petrified wood • **State reptile:** the Arizona ridge-nosed rattlesnake • **State motto:** "Ditat Deus," meaning "God enriches" • **State neckwear:** the bola tie • **State songs:** "Arizona March Song" and "Arizona" • **State mammal:** the ringtail

Some Famous Arizonans:

César Chávez (1927–1993), born on his family's farm near Yuma, was a community organizer, labor rights activist, and civil rights leader whose motto "Sí se puede" means "It can be done." Chávez founded the first successful farm workers union in 1962. His peaceful tactics—boycotts and hunger strikes—drew attention to the terrible working conditions of migrant workers, rallying millions to support his cause.

Charles Mingus (1922–1979), born in the border town of Nogales, was an acclaimed jazz musician, composer of "orchestral jazz," and band leader. His brilliant bass playing style made people think of that instrument in a new way. Mingus brought out the best in musicians who played alongside him. *Epitaph*, his longest jazz composition, premiered at Lincoln Center ten years after his death.

Sandra Day O'Connor (1930–) grew up on the Lazy B Ranch in southeastern Arizona. When she was six, she rode off alone on her horse, Chico, to check on a newborn calf. A rattlesnake spooked Chico, but little Sandra managed to hang on. That grit and determination served her well when she became the first female United States Supreme Court justice in 1981.

Linda Ronstadt (1946–) is a singer who was born in Tucson. She has been called the "Queen of Rock." Ronstadt grew up singing Mexican folk songs with her guitar-playing father, along with hits of the day with her siblings. She has sung rock, country, opera, pop, big band, and Mexican folk music. A versatile stylist, she interprets songs and makes them her own. To date, Ronstadt has received eleven Grammy® Awards. Forty-one of her albums have gone gold, platinum, or multi-platinum.

Louis Tewanima (c. 1888–1969), born in Second Mesa on the Hopi Reservation, used to run more than 100 miles to Winslow and back, to watch the trains go by. Sent to Carlisle Indian Boarding School in Pennsylvania, he excelled at long distance running. Tewanima competed at the Olympic Games twice, earning a silver medal in the 10,000 meters in 1912. His time of 32:06.6 set a U.S. record that remained unbroken for fifty-two years.

For Dawn Dixon, Erin Murphy, and Janni Lee Simner, who love Arizona as much as I do.

Many thanks to author Nancy Bo Flood, Brooke Gebow of The Nature Conservancy, Martin Kim at the Arizona State Museum, Gina Laczko and Wendy Weston at the Heard Museum, Sheilah Nicholas at the University of Arizona, Steele Wotkyns at the Lowell Observatory, and the Mammalogy and Ornithology Keepers at the Arizona-Sonora Desert Museum for their advice and assistance.
—J.J.S.

To Carrie Butler, who embodies the strength of Arizona women. Thank you for joining me on the adventures involved in creating this book! And to Mary Wong and Cathy Bonnell, two of my favorite supporters of children's books and book illustration in Arizona.
—L.A.

STERLING and the distinctive Sterling logo are registered trademarks of Sterling Publishing Co., Inc.

Library of Congress Cataloging-in-Publication Data
Stewart, Jennifer J.
The twelve days of Christmas in Arizona / written by Jennifer J. Stewart ; illustrated by Lynne Avril.   p. cm.
Summary: Isabella writes a letter home each of the twelve days she spends exploring Arizona at Christmastime, as her cousin Carlos shows her everything from a cactus wren in a palo verde tree to twelve Grand Canyon mules. Includes facts about Arizona.
ISBN 978-1-4027-7036-4
[1. Arizona—Fiction. 2. Christmas—Fiction. 3. Cousins—Fiction. 4. Hispanic Americans—Fiction. 5. Letters—Fiction.]
I. Avril, Lynne, 1951- ill. II. Title.   PZ7.S84895Tw 2010   [E] —dc22
2009034871

Lot#:
6 8 10 9 7 5
05/17

Published by Sterling Publishing Co., Inc.
1166 Avenue of the Americas, New York, NY 10036
Text © 2010 by Jennifer J. Stewart
Illustrations © 2010 by Lynne Avril
The original illustrations for this book were created using gouache and India ink.
Distributed in Canada by Sterling Publishing
c/o Canadian Manda Group, 664 Annette Street
Toronto, Ontario, Canada M6S 2C8
Distributed in the United Kingdom by GMC Distribution Services
Castle Place, 166 High Street, Lewes, East Sussex, England BN7 1XU
Distributed in Australia by Capricorn Link (Australia) Pty. Ltd.
P.O. Box 704, Windsor, NSW 2756, Australia

Manufactured in China
All rights reserved

The Grammy Awards® is a registered trademark of the National Academy of
Recording Arts & Sciences, Inc. All rights reserved.

ISBN 978-1-4027-7036-4

For information about custom editions, special sales, premium and corporate purchases, please contact
Sterling Special Sales Department at 800-805-5489 or specialsales@sterlingpublishing.com.

Designed by Kate Moll.

CANADA

Washington

Montana

Oregon

Idaho

Wyoming

Nevada

Utah

California

Colorado

Arizona

New Mexico

Alaska

Hawaii

(NOT TO SCALE)

MEXICO